Melly's Menorah

by Amye Rosenberg

BEHRMAN HOUSE

www.behrmanhouse.com

For Eric, Marina, Stefan, Sonia, and Nadia

Happy Hanukkah!

Design: Annemarie Redmond

Copyright © 1991, 2012 by Amye Rosenberg
Published by Behrman House, Inc.
Springfield, New Jersey 07081
www.behrmanhouse.com

ISBN: 978-0-87441-884-2
Printed in China

Library of Congress Cataloging-in-Publication Data
Rosenberg, Amye.
    Melly's menorah / by Amye Rosenberg.
        p. cm.
    ISBN 978-0-87441-884-2
  1. Hanukkah stories. 2. Menorah--Juvenile fiction. I. Title.
    BM695.H3R59 2012
    296.4'35--dc23
                                        2012019336

It was winter. The Gopher family had just moved into
their new home. The last boxes had been unpacked, and
everything was in its new place.

"Just think," said Mom. "Soon we will celebrate
Hanukkah in our new home."

"Yippee!" cried the Gopher children—Benny, Tess, and
little Melly.

One morning, little Melly noticed Benny busily sweeping the floor.

"Why are you doing that?" asked Melly.

"Tonight is the first night of Hanukkah," replied Benny. "I'm helping to get ready."

"Can I help too?" asked Melly excitedly.

"No," teased Benny. "You're better at messing up the house."

Tess was in the next room, making things with colored paper.

"What are you doing?" asked Melly.

"I'm going to decorate the entire house for Hanukkah,"
replied Tess.

"Even the bathroom?" asked Melly.

"Don't be silly!" said Tess with a laugh.

Melly was serious. "If no one will decorate the bathroom for Hanukkah, I will," she thought. She headed for the bathroom.

Melly peeked in. Mom was sitting on the bathroom floor amid rolls of wrapping paper. "What are you doing?" Melly asked.

"I'm trying to wrap these presents where no one will see them," said Mom.

"Can I help?" asked Melly.

"No," said Mom. "Then your presents won't be a surprise!"

Melly went to her room.
She wished she had
presents to wrap for everyone.

"I know," she thought. "I'll
make Hanukkah cards."

She was cutting and
coloring when Dad burst
in with the vacuum cleaner
whirring loudly.

"We've got to clean up
this mess," declared Dad.
"Company is coming tonight
for Hanukkah."

"I'm making Hanukkah cards," said Melly.

But Dad could not hear her over the roar of the vacuum.

Suddenly every last scrap of paper was sucked up and gone forever. So much for Hanukkah cards. Melly would have to find something else to do.

It was then that Melly smelled something yummy. She followed her nose to the kitchen where Grandma was busily cooking.

"What are you doing?" asked Melly.

"I'm frying latkes. I'm making applesauce. I'm baking cookies."

"Can I help?" asked Melly.

"No," said Grandma. "But you can play with the leftover cookie dough."

9

"Since it is Hanukkah," Melly thought, "I'll make a menorah."

She rolled and patted and pinched the dough. In no time at all, she had made a lovely menorah, with eight candle holders and a special place for the *shamash*.

Grandpa came into the room and began rummaging in the cupboards.

"What are you doing?" asked Melly.

"I'm looking for the menorah," said Grandpa. "It's time to polish it for the first night of Hanukkah."

"I made a menorah," said Melly.

But Grandpa was so busy he took no notice. "Why don't you go out and play in the snow?" he said.

"I think I'll do just that," thought Melly, "since no one will let me help get ready for Hanukkah."

Melly passed through the kitchen on her way out the door.

A sheet of Hanukkah cookies sat on the table, ready for baking. Melly grinned. She placed her cookie-dough menorah among them.

Grandma whisked the cookie sheet into the oven without noticing a thing.

Melly put on her jacket and boots and slipped outside.

The front yard was covered with snow. Melly decided to make up a game. First she made a pile of snowballs. Then, one by one, she tossed them over her shoulder and tried to guess where they landed. One snowball landed with an odd thud.

"Ouch! Is that any way to greet your Uncle Jack?"
Melly turned around. "Sorry." She blushed.

Uncle Jack just laughed. He scooped up Melly into an armload
of gifts and carried her into the house.

Soon the other guests arrived with presents and treats to share. The house was festive with decorations, gaily wrapped gifts, and the merry chatter of children.

"I want to light the first candle!" squealed Melly.

"I want to open the first present," cried Tess.

"I want to eat the first latke!" boomed Benny.

"I want us all to have a happy Hanukkah!" said Uncle Jack.

Just then, Grandpa rushed into the room. "I have terrible news," he announced. "The menorah is nowhere to be found. I've searched everywhere. It must have gotten lost when we moved!"

"How will we light the candles?" asked Tess.

"We can't have Hanukkah without a menorah," moaned Mom. Suddenly the joy was gone. Everyone was silent and sad.

"Wait!" cried Melly. "I know where there's a menorah!"

She raced into the kitchen and looked around. Grandma's special Hanukkah cookies were piled high on a shining silver tray. There, among them, was Melly's menorah, now baked golden brown.

Melly grabbed it and returned as fast as she could.

Everyone gathered around the cookie-dough menorah.

"Look at that," roared Grandpa. "Melly's made a menorah!"

"Oh my." Grandma laughed when she saw it. "We could have eaten it!"

"It is a bit unusual," said Dad. "But it is a menorah."

"I think it's the most beautiful menorah I've ever seen," said Mom. She helped Melly light the first candle.

"Happy Hanukkah! Hooray for Melly!" they all cheered.

Then everyone had a fine feast of Grandma's latkes. They opened presents, played spin-the-dreidel, and sang songs of celebration.

And so, on each of the eight nights of Hanukkah, Melly's cookie-dough menorah glowed proudly—and so did Melly.

Without her, there would have been no first Hanukkah to celebrate in the Gophers' new home.

HANUKKAH WORDS

HANUKKAH

This joyful holiday is a celebration of our religious freedom. We play games, sing songs, give gifts, and light the menorah. Hanukkah is also called the Festival of Lights.

MENORAH

The Hanukkah menorah is a special candleholder with eight candles—one for each of the eight nights of Hanukkah—and an extra candle called the *shamash*.

SHAMASH

The *shamash* is a special candle. It sits proudly above all the others because it has an important job to do. It is used to light all the other candles on the menorah.

DREIDEL

A dreidel is a four-sided top with which we play Hanukkah games.

LATKES

These are Hanukkah pancakes made from potatoes. When they are eaten with applesauce or sour cream, they are especially delicious!

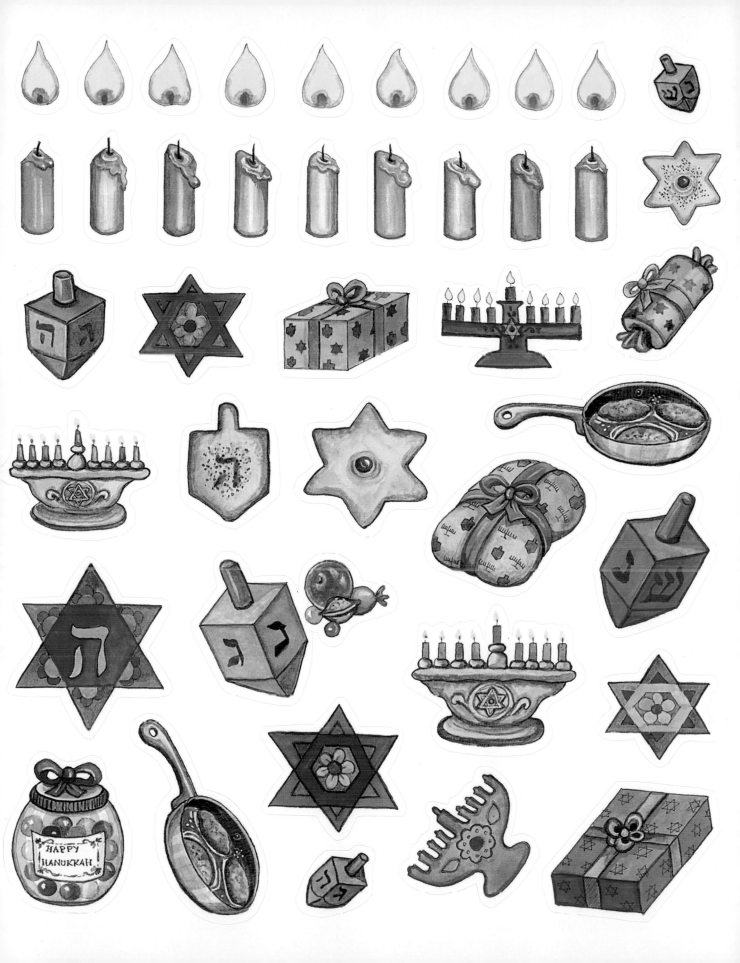